# A modern approach

Reading and writing should flow through the natural activities and interests of the child. The next most important aid is a series of books designed to stimulate and interest him and to give daily practice at the right level.

Educational experts from five Caribbean countries have co-operated with the author to design and produce this Ladybird Sunstart Reading Scheme. Their work has been influenced by (a) the widely accepted piece of research *Key Words to Literacy*[1], a word list which is adapted here for tropical countries and used to accelerate learning in the early stages; and (b) the work of Dr. Dennis Craig[2] of the School of Education, U.W.I., and other specialists who have carried out research in areas where the English language is being taught to young children whose natural speech on entering school is a patois or dialect varying considerably from standard English.

[1] Key Words to Literacy *by J McNally and W Murray,* published by The Teacher Publishi~~~ ~ Derbyshire House, Kette

[2] An experiment in teachir *Caribbean Universities Pr Journal of the Ministry of*

**THE LADYBIRD SUNSTART READING SCHEME** consists of six books and three workbooks. These are graded and written with a controlled vocabulary and plentiful repetition. They are fully illustrated.

Book 1 'Lucky dip' (for beginners) is followed by Book 2 'On the beach'. Workbook A is parallel to these and covers the vocabulary of both books. The workbook reinforces the words learned in the readers, teaches handwriting and introduces phonic training.

Book 3 'The kite' and Book 4 'Animals, birds and fish' follow Books 1 and 2, and are supported by Workbook B. This reinforces the vocabulary of Books 3 and 4 and again contains handwriting exercises and phonic training.

Book 5 'I wish' and Book 6 'Guess what?' with Workbook C complete the scheme.

The illustrated handbook (free) for parents and teachers is entitled 'A Guide to the Teaching of Reading'.

For classroom use there are two boxes of large flash cards which cover the first three books.

Published by Ladybird Books Ltd Loughborough Leicestershire UK
Ladybird Books Inc Auburn Maine 04210 USA

© LADYBIRD BOOKS LTD MCMLXXIV
*All rights reserved. No part of this publication may be reproduced, stored in a retrieval system, or transmitted in any form or by any means, electronic, mechanical, photo-copying, recording or otherwise, without the prior consent of the copyright owner.*

Printed in England

**BOOK 1**
The Ladybird SUNSTART Reading Scheme
*(a 'Key Words' Reading Scheme)*

# Lucky dip

*by* W. MURRAY
*with illustrations*
*by* MARTIN AITCHISON

Ladybird Books  Loughborough
in collaboration with Longman Caribbean Ltd

# Talk about the picture

4

# Tell the story

(1)

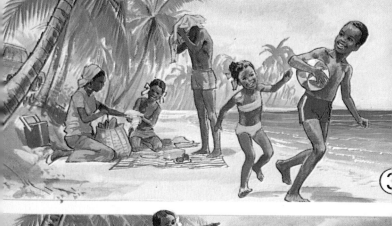

(3)

6

(5)

# Talk about the pictures

# Learning colours

**LOOK** and find
another like this

and this

and this

and this

boy    girl    bird

boy     man     box

girl     a girl     boy     a boy

a girl
a boy

new words     a     girl     boy

a girl          a boy

a girl

and

a boy

---

new word          and

I see a boy

and

I see a girl.

big girl  little girl  big boy  little boy

I see
a big girl.
I see
a little boy.

new words     big     little

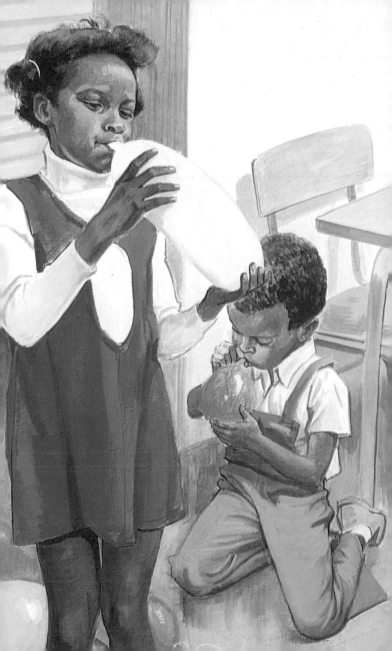

big boy     big girl     little boy     little gir

You see
the big boy
and
you see
the little girl.

new words     You     you     the

the boy  the girl  a bird

You see
the little boy
and
the big girl.
You see
a bird.

new word       bird

tree

a tree

the tree

Look at
the tree.
Look at
the big tree.
Look at
the little bird.

new words    Look    at    tree

# 2
two

Look at the boy
in the big tree.

You see two birds
in the big tree.

The boy sees the birds
and the two birds
see the boy.

A boy is in
the big tree.

A girl is in
the little tree.

is

Come and see.

You come and
see it.

Come and see
the Lucky dip.

---

new words    Come     come     it

**1**

one

**2**

two

You see one bird.

You see one girl.

You see two boys.

The two boys look
at the bird.

Look at that.

Can you see that?

That is it.

That is the Lucky dip.

new words    that     That     Can

The girl comes.

She comes to look.

She can see it.

Can you see it?

Can you see
the Lucky dip?

Lucky
dip

The boy comes.

He comes to look.

He can see it.

You can see it.

box

The boy and the girl want a box.

He says, I want a box.

She says, I want a box

new words   want   box   says

Lu
dip

a man

The girl says to the man
I want a box, please.

One for you,
the man says.

---

new words    man    please    for

Lucky

Thank you, says the gi
to the man. Thank you.

Look, she says
to the boy.

Look at that.

---

Thank

The boy says to the man
I want a box, please.

One for you,
the man says.

Thank you, says the bo
to the man. Thank you.

Look, he says
to the girl.

Look at that.

# Words used in this book

Cover: Lucky dip

**Total number of words 34**